KATE PUGSLEY
MERMAID DREAMS

tundra

Maya loves the beach.

The air smells fresh and salty.

The sand feels warm and soft
between her toes.

Maya and her parents settle into a spot near the ocean.

"Will you play with me?" Maya asks.

"Maybe later. We want to relax now," says Mom.

"Why don't you make some new friends?" says Dad.

From her turtle floaty, Maya watches the other kids having fun, but she is too shy to say hello.

Maya listens to the waves flow in and out.

She wonders what it's like deep down on the ocean floor.

Her eyes grow heavy and she closes them against the sun's bright rays.

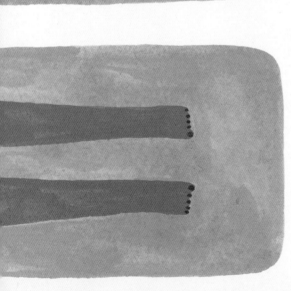

Maya suddenly feels a cool breeze against her face.

She is riding the waves on her turtle's back!

The water sparkles like jewels.

Maya and her turtle dive below the surface,

swimming down,

down,

down.

At the bottom of the ocean, she discovers
a secret underwater world!

Maya slides off her turtle and realizes she can swim just like the other ocean dwellers.

She's a mermaid with a beautiful blue tail!

Maya hears a voice floating out from the coral:

HELLO!

She spots the glimmer of a yellow tail.
Who could that be?

When she swims closer, she sees . . .

. . . it's only a fish!

Its scales are sparkly, but its personality is dull.

Maya hears the voice again:

OVER HERE!

She spots two eyes peering out from behind
the coral. She swims to the reef to discover . . .

. . . the eyes belong to an octopus!

It has eight wonderful legs, but it can't hold a conversation.

Maya hears a giggle: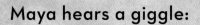

HEE HEE HEE!

She sees bubbles rising up from behind the rocks.
She follows the trail and swims right into . . .

. . . a herd of seahorses!

They're silly, but they can't laugh at her jokes.

Then Maya sees an unusual
shape in the distance. It floats
closer and closer . . .

It's another mermaid!

"You found me!"
the mermaid says.

"It's your turn to hide now," says the friendly mermaid.

"1 . . . 2 . . . 3 . . ."

Maya swims into the underwater jungle.

She finds the perfect hiding spot.

Her eyes grow heavy watching the seaweed
move with the current . . .

"Got you!"

Maya hears a familiar voice and looks up sleepily.

"Hi, I'm Pearl. Do you want to play with me?"

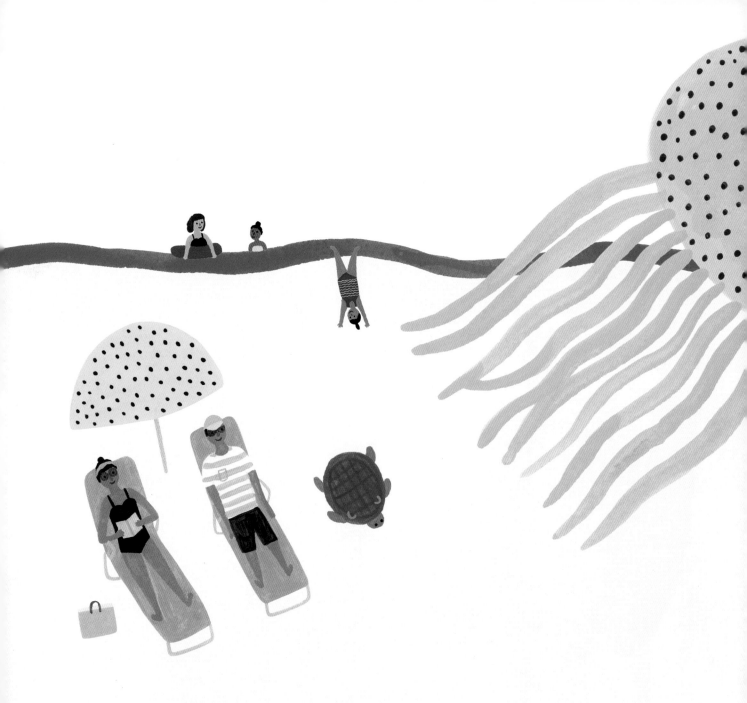

"I always want to play!" exclaims Maya.

"Let's pretend we're mermaids," whispers Pearl.

And that's exactly what they did.

For my dear sister, Tess

Tundra Books, an imprint of Penguin Random House Canada Young Readers,
a Penguin Random House Company

Library and Archives Canada Cataloguing in Publication

Pugsley, Kate, author, illustrator
    Mermaid dreams / Kate Pugsley.

Issued in print and electronic formats.

ISBN 978-0-7352-6491-5 (hardcover).—ISBN 978-0-7352-6492-2 (ebook)

    I. Title.

PZ7.1.P84Mer 2019   j813'.6   C2018-900675-7
                                            C2018-900676-5

Published simultaneously in the United States of America by Tundra Books of
Northern New York, an imprint of Penguin Random House Canada Young Readers,
a Penguin Random House Company

Library of Congress Control Number: 2018936942

Acquired by Tara Walker and Elizabeth Kribs
Edited by Elizabeth Kribs
Designed by John Martz
The artwork in this book was made with gouache and
colored pencil and assembled digitally.
The text was set in Neutraface 2.

Printed and bound in China

www.penguinrandomhouse.ca

1   2   3   4   5   23   22   21   20   19

Penguin
Random House
tundra | TUNDRA BOOKS